# PRESENTS FOR LUPE

*By Dorothy P. Lathrop*

# PRESENTS FOR LUPE

## DOROTHY P. LATHROP

### THE MACMILLAN COMPANY
NEW YORK
1940

13682
1/7/41

OCLC # 1814782

*Designed and printed in the*
*United States of America by*
PACE PRESS INCORPORATED

*To*

ANNE CARROLL MOORE

whose enthusiasm for children's books
is boundless and contagious and the
inspiration of all who make them

# PRESENTS FOR LUPE

Lupe was a little red squirrel from South America.

It was John and Joan, the twins, who named her. It made them feel more acquainted with her—almost as if she belonged to them.

But she didn't. Lupe lived in a tiny cage in a pet-shop window, and all day long she ate sunflower seeds and slept. There was nothing else for her to do. She slept in a corner, with her forehead on the floor of the cage and her nose tucked between her paws. She looked very uncomfortable and very lonesome.

Every day on their way to school the twins stared into the window as they hurried past. And every day on their way home they stopped for a long time and watched her.

But Lupe never looked at them. She no longer cared how many people passed her window. Sometimes the children tapped on the glass. But Lupe was used to that noise and just went on cracking sunflower seeds.

"Lupe! Lupe!" they called. Perhaps she couldn't hear through the glass, or maybe she didn't know yet that that was her name.

Every day at home Joan and John talked about the little red squirrel to whoever would listen.

"Nobody has bought her yet," said John hopefully.

"Her cage is too small for her," said Joan. "She can only take two steps, and then she has to turn around. And her tail sticks out through the bars."

"She can't ever run," said John.

"It's a beautiful bushy tail," Joan went on. "It's black, and then orange, and then black again right at the tip."

"We wish she was ours!" said the twins together.

But many days passed, and all that time Lupe was turning around and around in her tiny cage, eating sunflower seeds and sleeping, then eating and going to sleep again to pass the time away.

"I could build her a big cage," said John, "so she could run."

So he did, and Joan helped him. Each day they went to make sure Lupe was still there. When it was finished it was so big it took both of them to lift it.

"It's done!" cried John at last. "It's all ready for Lupe!"

"Oh, please!" begged Joan. "She'd like living with us."

That very day Lupe did come to live with them. But she felt very strange in this new, big cage. She walked around it with her tail held tightly up over her back as if she was trying to hide under it. She stiffened her legs all ready to jump if she met any dreadful thing in the corners, and she grunted as she walked.

"Does she mean that for growling?" asked Joan anxiously.

"I guess so. That's what she did when I felt of her fur. It's sort of stiff when you smooth it the wrong way, isn't it?"

"She wouldn't let *me*. Why is she scared of *us*?" mourned Joan.

Lupe was running, but slowly for fear she would bump her nose. She was so pleased at having room to run that soon her tail, which had been scared up over her back, arched out behind.

"She *can* run in her cage!" cried John proudly.

But when Lupe, tired of running, had eaten a few sunflower seeds and tucked her head between her toes on the bare cage floor, she still looked uncomfortable and she still looked lonesome.

"Do you suppose she's homesick for South America?" worried Joan.

"I don't know," said John. "But maybe if we brought her some presents from there, she'd feel more at home."

But where could they get any? They asked everyone. And soon lots of packages began to come for Lupe. It was just like Christmas!

D.P.Lathrop

And every package held presents from South America.

In the first were some ears of corn, because corn grew in that country before it grew anywhere else in the world. But it didn't make John think of South America, and he was afraid Lupe would be disappointed too. But Joan said politely that she was sure Lupe would like such *fancy* corn. For it wasn't plain yellow. One ear was all mottled, and one was almost the color of Lupe's red fur, and another as black as the underside of her tail.

Lupe grunted suspiciously when they put it in her cage.

"Say 'thank you,' Lupe," reproved Joan. "It's a present."

Cautiously Lupe smelled of it, then reached for it with arms stretched thin. Her strong teeth tore off the kernels, but out of each she nibbled only the little heart. She wasn't hungry, but ripping them off was fun! Faster and faster the kernels flew until they pattered around her like hail and the cobs were almost bare.

"She liked that present all right!" said John.

"But do you think she'll like this one?" asked Joan doubtfully, looking at a little brown bowl that had been made by the Indians.

"Maybe, if we put her sunflower seeds in it so she won't step on them."

So they did, for Lupe never seemed to like her food much after she had walked on it. And there she sat by her bowl as proudly as if she had always eaten out of dishes, cracking the seeds, eating them, and throwing the husks down in a neat little pile beside her.

She never knew what she would find in her bowl, for the twins thought she must be awfully tired of *just* sunflower seeds. So sometimes it was hickory nuts, sometimes pecans or filberts. But whenever she found little sweet Indian nuts, her tail twitched with pleasure and, pushing everything else aside with her nose, she pulled those out first. And always there were big pieces of apple. Never in the pet shop had she had so many good things to eat.

"Oh, look!" cried Joan. "Her teeth are red like her fur!"

But how thirsty dry nuts made Lupe! Every morning and every night Joan washed out her drinking cup and filled it up again.

One day Lupe found her water in a new little green glass cup.

"Uncle John says it's from Mexico, but he can't find a glass from South America so please let Lupe drink out of it," said John.

Lupe didn't care where it came from as long as it held fresh, cold water. And the twins liked it because it made her head pale green when they saw it through the glass. They could see her little tongue, too, flicking in and out, and hear the tiny sound it made when she drank, like raindrops falling.

"Here's another present for Lupe!" cried John, unwrapping a big rough ball that was heavy and that rattled. "But what is it?"

It looked like a nut, but it was bigger than any the twins had ever seen. John had to know what was inside. But it was Lupe's present, and it seemed only polite to let her open it herself.

Lupe willingly set to work on it. How loudly her teeth rasped! Surely at that rate she would be through the shell in no time!

But she gnawed and gnawed. Then she hugged the big ball harder and gnawed again. What was the matter?

"Try again, Lupe," urged John.

But Lupe wouldn't. Her teeth had only scraped a white place on the shell—no hole at all!

"Then I'll open it!" he said, and took it out and hit it with a hammer. But the hammer only bounced. He hit it harder. The hammer bounced again, and so did the nut.

"I didn't know it was so hard." . . . BANG. . . . "No wonder Lupe couldn't make a hole in it"—BANG—"with her little teeth!"

But neither could John with his hammer. It was his father who, with a chisel, uncovered the nuts, all closely fitted together inside.

"Brazil nuts!" shouted the twins. "Is *that* how they grow!"

Lupe stretched up on her hind legs and looked in too. Brazil nuts! She knew what to do about those!

There was something Lupe wanted and for which she hunted restlessly all over her cage. Didn't she have everything a squirrel could want, everything except freedom to run in the treetops?

She had more nuts than she needed, cracked and easy to eat, and whole ones to gnaw on to keep her teeth from growing too long. These she tucked into corners and banged in hard with her nose.

No use! She couldn't jam them down out of sight! Would anyone steal them before she was hungry enough to eat them herself?

How could she be hungry? All the squash and melon seeds were saved for her, too. John even gave her those from his apples, but Lupe thought *they* were almost too small to bother with.

It wasn't food for which she was hunting. But she did taste the nasturtiums sent her because they, also, grew in her country before they blossomed in our gardens. But if they weren't food for squirrels, what good were they? She left them in tatters.

Often, shutting all the windows and doors, the twins let her loose in the room. How she loved that! But she had to find out what everything was, and thought that only her mouth could tell her. And how grownups hate to find nips out of chair legs!

But back in her cage, before she curled herself up for sleep, she still hunted for that thing she couldn't find anywhere.

"More and more and *more* presents for Lupe!" cried Joan one day, dumping an armful of packages on the floor.

Lupe stood up on her hind legs and peered out through the wire, first through this square and then through that.

"*She* wants to see too," said John.

So they let her out, and she circled among the packages; but always just out of reach, for she hated to be picked up. Her smooth back slid from under their fingers like quicksilver.

"I wish she'd let me hold her," said Joan wistfully.

"She isn't as scared as she was," said John, undoing a package.

But at the sharp rattle of paper Lupe leaped across the room in a fright, every hair on her tail standing out by itself. Scared? She couldn't have run faster if she had been chased by a cat!

"Lupe! Lupe, come back! Here's your present," Joan called.

"Why, it's just a pineapple!" cried John. "Did everything grow in South America first?"

"Never mind; maybe you won't know what this is," said Joan, trying to be very quiet with the paper because of Lupe.

And John didn't. It was a little round fruit, as brown and rough as a potato.

" 'This is a sapodilla,' " read the twins. " 'Lupe probably calls it a dilly for short. Everybody does'."

"What's this?" asked John, pulling out what looked like a melon.

"'A papaya,'" read Joan.

Next they unwrapped a sicana, a fruit as long and as round and as red as a Bologna, but which smelled like sweet spices. And in the last package was something as fragrant as a flower, called a ceriman, that looked like a big banana covered with green armor.

Lupe ran around sniffing and taking nips out of everything.

"Wait, Lupe!" cried Joan. "We want to taste of them, too."

So she cut pieces for all three. They sampled each fruit, and Lupe flitted from this piece to that, flicking her tail joyfully.

The dilly tasted like gritty wet sugar; the sicana, as spicy and sweet as it smelled. It had seeds like a watermelon, and Lupe ate all she could find. But the twins liked the little black seeds of the papaya, because they tasted just like those of nasturtiums. And the ceriman, when they lifted off its scales, was the most delicious of all, even though it didn't come quite all the way from South America like the rest. Neither did apples, but they, Lupe thought, were better than anything else. So she jumped in her cage and ate a big piece, peeling it first with her teeth as neatly as with a knife.

How juicy the fruits were! Everyone had to wash up. The twins scrubbed their hands and faces, but Lupe washed even her back.

One present Lupe simply hated. But Joan thought it was pretty, and that it would be very becoming to Lupe. How could anything make her more beautiful than she was in her own shining red and black fur? And who ever heard of a squirrel's necklace?

This one was made of strange nutshells. It just fitted Lupe's neck; but the shells were big, because they were part of a necklace an Indian had made for himself. They clinked together in a way he had loved to hear, but which terrified Lupe.

Joan wanted to see how it looked, so John caught and held Lupe while Joan tied it around her neck. How lucky that she was gentle and tame, and that she never bit! Those teeth, sharp as chisels, could easily make holes in hard nuts. What about soft fingers? No, Lupe only wiggled and scrambled with claws as sharp as a kitten's.

"Hurry up! Ouch! I can't hold her!"

Lupe slipped through John's fingers as if she were buttered, and flew across the room with every shell jingling. The faster she ran the louder they clattered, and nowhere could she escape them. Luckily the cord wasn't tied very well, and off they slipped.

"I didn't even see how it looked," wailed Joan.

And she never did, for when Lupe had finished with the necklace there wasn't enough left of any one shell to tie to another.

One morning a letter came for the twins, and a package for Lupe.

"Here," said the letter, "are some animals from Lupe's own land to keep her company. But don't ask *me* what they are. Ask the Indian who made them or, better still, ask Lupe."

They were three very queer-looking creatures. Two were made of pottery the color of earth, and had patterns painted on their backs like blankets. The twins looked at the biggest one doubtfully.

"It's a kangaroo," said John.

"It's a squirrel," said Joan. "Kangaroos' tails stick out behind when they sit down. They don't hold them up their backs like that."

"It doesn't look much like Lupe," said John, "but maybe that Indian never saw a squirrel close to."

Perhaps that wasn't the Indian's fault if all squirrels were like Lupe. *She* hardly ever sat still for a minute, or stopped skipping about even long enough for John to count her whiskers.

"It's holding a nut in its paws, so it must be a squirrel."

"*Is* it a nut? Let's ask Lupe."

So they put the strange animal in her cage and waited to see what would happen.

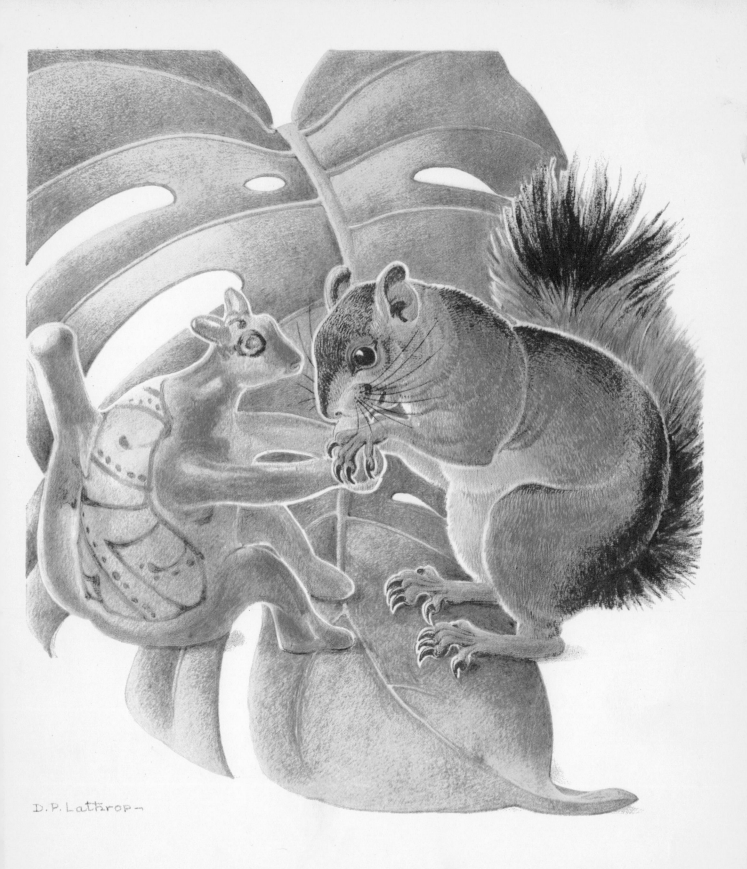

And Lupe, flicking her tail with curiosity, reached out her thin little hands with all eight fingers spread wide, seized the other creature, and began to gnaw the thing it was holding.

"See, *Lupe* thinks it's a nut!" cried Joan in delight.

If it was, it was not worth opening. Lupe bit the animal's ear, but it wouldn't fight back. It didn't even run away. Why, it was a squirrel not worth the biting! So she toppled it over on its clay side and, turning her back, got a real nut out of her bowl.

She wouldn't even turn around to look at the smallest animal.

"I think it's a baby bird waiting for a worm," said Joan, "and flapping its wings."

"*I* think it's a toad with its mouth wide open—or a frog."

But neither of them were sure what the third creature was.

"A fox," said John.

"A dog," said Joan.

But their father said that it must be a coati. Didn't they see the rings on its tail? Besides, it had a long body, short legs, and a little sharp, pointed face. But the twins had never seen a coati.

Lupe didn't care *what* it was. Even the big green leaf that was almost like some that grew in her own jungle did not make her feel at home. Nor did it keep her from running back and forth hunting, hunting, hunting for something she wanted very badly.

"Are you sure this is for Lupe?" asked Joan wistfully, when she opened still another bundle the postman had brought.

For in it was a doll—not an ordinary one, but a queer one made of husks. Many times Joan's mother had told her of the cornhusk dolls her grandmother used to make her. But these husks never grew around corn. These felt like velvet.

Even John, who scorned all dolls, looked curiously at this one. For this was an Indian, and a chief. His chest was broad, the muscles on his legs bulged, and only a neck as stiff as his could have held aloft such a towering headdress. Feathers waved above his brow and hung from his belt. He was very proud.

"If it comes from South America," replied John, "of course it's Lupe's."

So Joan put it in the cage, though she was sure she wanted it more than Lupe did. How could a squirrel play with a doll?

Lupe, too, wondered. But she was very inquisitive. She thought it must be good for *something*. So she smelled it, bit it, and carried it around. Then she tore a piece out of it and tasted it.

"Oh, Lupe!" protested Joan.

No, it was good for nothing at all, so she dropped it among the nutshells Joan hadn't yet swept out of the cage that day.

What queer things people sent to make a squirrel happy!

There was the little round box that was really a gourd all carved and painted with pictures. People and llamas and monkeys marched all the way around it, and birds sat among the strange flowers.

But Lupe didn't care about the outside. She wanted to know what was *inside*. So she peered in.

It was empty! Nor was the box itself good to eat. She tried it.

Then there was the big ivory nut. In South America they cut buttons from it—buttons that do look just like ivory.

But Lupe didn't need any buttons. Her coat was all in one piece.

And there were the little brown cacao beans.

But Lupe didn't want to make any cocoa. She didn't like it.

There were flowers, also—a begonia; and a flower that looked like a small flat calla lily, but wasn't; and a great yellow sunflower, too, because its ancestors grew in Lupe's land very long ago.

"*That's* why Lupe likes sunflower seeds so much!"

But there were other things that did make Lupe happy. Peanuts, for one. Of these she left only the shells. She wasn't allowed to have very many of them, even if they did grow first down there. Other nuts, said the twins' father, were better for squirrels.

And there were paradise nuts, brown and deeply grooved, from tall trees in the dense forests. These Lupe ate as if never had she tasted anything more delicious. She sat right there until she had finished a whole one, her twitching tail signaling her pleasure.

But nothing that anyone brought her seemed to make her feel really at home, or even happy for long.

"I wish I knew what she wanted," said Joan sadly.

Then one day someone brought her a big gourd. That, too, was all covered with pictures, but the twins knew that she wouldn't care about those. And what *could* she do with the gourd?

"Shall we give it to her?" asked Joan doubtfully.

"It's hers," said John firmly, and he put it in her cage.

"Soon there won't be room for Lupe," said Joan.

The gourd rocked a little as John set it down, and Lupe eyed it suspiciously. Was it alive? What was this big black thing? It wasn't a cat, was it? Lupe opened her mouth wide and scolded loudly, lashing her tail up and down to show she wasn't afraid of anything. Her ears lay close to her head and her sides heaved.

She looked so funny the twins sat and laughed. Lupe was affronted, and soon her harsh scolding died down to a mutter. She stretched out her neck very cautiously as far as she could.

Her legs she left far behind for safety. The gourd didn't move, though her nose almost touched it. Why, it was nothing to be afraid of! She circled about it, then reached up to examine every bit of it.

There was a hole in the top. Lupe stuck her head in and looked down into the darkness. Her tail fairly danced with excitement. She stood on her tiptoes and leaned over until her head disappeared. There was a scramble, and *all* of her vanished.

"Lupe's inside!" shrieked Joan.

The gourd rocked wildly as Lupe turned around and around exploring it. The tip of her tail stuck out, was gone, then waved gaily.

Now up popped her head.

"She's a jack-in-the-box!" cried John.

Now there wasn't a sign of her, head or tail. Nor was there a sound. The gourd stood perfectly still.

"Why, that's what Lupe wanted," said Joan. "She wanted a house."

But soon Lupe's head bobbed up again, and she peered all about her. Even yet she wasn't quite satisfied. She had a house, but she wanted something more.

She jumped out. She seized the Indian doll, and before Joan could stop her began tearing it to bits. It was dreadful to hear it rip!

In less than a minute what had once been a chief, haughty in his headdress of feathers, was only a pile of shredded, velvety husks.

These Lupe raked into her arms and pushed into her wide-open mouth until it could stretch no farther. The husks stuck out stiffly on both sides like fierce and enormous whiskers! Mouthful after great mouthful she stuffed into her house. Back and forth she darted busily until not a shred of the doll was left outside.

"Oh, dear!" mourned Joan. "It was a lovely doll!"

Then the bed had to be made. Lupe patted it, and pulled it, and stirred it all around. She worked so hard that the gourd teetered from side to side. And though the twins couldn't see what was happening, they heard the faint, muffled rustle of the husks. Sometimes Lupe's head stuck out for a minute, and sometimes her tail.

At last the bed was made.

"Why didn't we think of giving her a house?" asked John. "*We* live in a house."

"And a bed?" asked Joan. "I wouldn't like to sleep on the floor."

"Here she comes out again."

For Lupe had forgotten something.

She picked up one of the nuts she had tried in vain to bury out of sight in the corner, and carried it into her house. Out she whisked and got another. One by one she carried them all in, big ones and little ones. For at last she had a place to store them.

Lupe had set up housekeeping. And at last she was happy. She looked out of her house, her eyes shining proudly.

Then she settled down deep in her soft bed with the walls of her house protectingly around her, and went comfortably to sleep.